Children's Room

JUL 19 1989

DATE DUE

w/ Christmas books

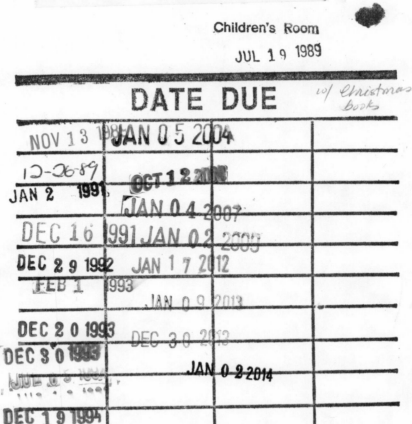

NOV 13 198	JAN 0 5 2004	
12-26-89	OCT 1 2 200	
JAN 2 1991	JAN 0 4 2007	
DEC 16 991	JAN 0 2 2009	
DEC 2 9 1992	JAN 1 7 2012	
FEB 1 1993	JAN 0 9 2013	
DEC 2 0 1993	DEC 3 0 2013	
DEC 3 0 1993	JAN 0 2 2014	
JUL 0 5 1994		
DEC 1 9 1994		
DEC 2 - 1995		
JAN 1 0 1998		
JAN 1 1 2001		
JAN 1 4 2002		

LITTLE BEAR'S
CHRISTMAS

by Janice
Pictures by Mariana

LOTHROP, LEE & SHEPARD CO., NEW YORK

16   17   18   19   20   21   22   23   24   25

It was winter and Little Bear was fast asleep in his snug little house, dreaming of spring. He dreamed that he was walking in the woods sniffing the delicious spring air. The spring air smelled of HONEY!

Little Bear's mouth watered. He wanted to taste the honey so much that his nose began to twitch. It twitched so hard that his eyes flew open and he was awake. Wide awake and very hungry.

"Is it spring?" he asked. But nobody answered. So he got out of bed to see for himself. He went to the window and looked out. There was a great big yellow moon shining. The ground and trees were covered with shining snow, and away off in the village all the houses were lighted up and shining.

Little Bear's eyes grew round as saucers. He had never seen anything like *this* before.

"I wonder what it can be?" he said. And he got dressed and went outside.

Little Bear looked around at all the shining whiteness. Then he picked up some snow and tasted it.

"Delicious!" said Little Bear, and he started to walk through the woods toward the village.

When he got there, the windows and doors of every house had wreaths of holly. Some were tied with scarlet ribbons, others with wide silver ribbons. There were trees both outside and inside the houses, all covered with shining colored balls and little silver bells. Little Bear had never seen anything like *this* before.

"I'm so glad I woke up," he said.

Children were skating on the frozen pond, laughing and shouting.

"Hi, Little Bear," they called. "Did you wake up for Christmas?"

"Christmas? What's that?" asked Little Bear.

The children looked surprised.

"Don't you know what *Christmas* is, Little Bear? Why, Christmas is the best day in the whole year. You write to Santa Claus to tell him what you want and on Christmas eve he brings it to you on his sleigh, and you find it in your stocking on Christmas morning. That's what Christmas is," said a little boy.

"Can I write to Santa Claus, too?"
asked Little Bear.

"Of course! Anyone can write to
him. But hurry—it's nearly time for Santa
to start out with his presents now. And
don't forget to hang up your stocking in
front of the chimney."

Little Bear hurried back to his house to write his letter.

DEAR MR SANTA CLAUS
I AM A LITTLE BEAR AND I
HAVE NEVER HAD CHRISTMAS
PLEAS BRING ME SOME CHRISTMAS
YOURS TRULY
LITTLE BEAR

Little Bear mailed his letter, and hung up six stockings. Then he sat down by the chimney to wait.

At midnight sharp he heard a noise in the chimney—a panting and puffing noise.

"Who's there?" cried Little Bear.

"It's Santa Claus," said a jolly voice. "I'm stuck. Catch hold of my legs and help me down."

"Just a minute!" said Little Bear. He pulled and tugged until at last Santa Claus came tumbling down the chimney.

"Thank you, Little Bear," Santa Claus said when he had caught his breath. "That's a mighty narrow chimney you've got. Let me see now...your letter says that you would like to have some Christmas." His eyes twinkled.

"Yes, please," said Little Bear.

Santa Claus stroked his beard and thought for a while.

"Well now, let's see...the best way to have Christmas?" He thought some more and then said, "How would you like to ride with me tonight? And take presents to children?"

"Oh, yes! I'd like that!" shouted Little Bear.

"Just put on this coat and cap," said Santa, "and jump into my sleigh. My reindeer will take us to the houses of the children on this list, and you can climb down the chimney and fill up the stockings at these six houses. Here are the letters. But be sure and put the right presents into the right stockings."

"Oh, that's easy!" said Little Bear.

So Little Bear climbed into the sleigh.
"Mr. Dingle's house, please!" said
Santa to the reindeer. And off they went
with a jingle of sleigh bells.

When they got to Mr. Dingle's house, Little Bear climbed down the chimney. He read the letter from Flossie Dingle, then took a beautiful French doll out of

Santa's sack and put it carefully into Flossie Dingle's stocking. Then he climbed up the chimney again.

"Mr. Smith's house, please," Santa said to the reindeer. And off they went with the sleigh bells jingling.

Little Bear left a sled and a party dress for Tony and Lydia Smith. Then Santa said, "Mr. Brown's house, please." And after that, "Mr. Johnson's house," until they had visited all six houses on the list.

Then the reindeer flew back to Little
Bear's house and let him off on the roof.

And before Little Bear could say
"Thank you," and "Merry Christmas,"
Santa had disappeared.

Little Bear climbed down his chimney. "Chimneys are so much nicer than doors," he said.

Then he gave a little shout. For there, in the middle of the room, was a great big Christmas tree, all decorated with red and white peppermint sticks and nuts and ginger cookies and bunches of raisins.

The table was set, and sitting around
it were his special friends—Owl and Sparrow and Squirrel and Squeaky the mouse.

"Merry Christmas, Little Bear!" they sang out. "Santa invited us to your party," Squeaky added, "and he said to tell you to be sure to look in your stockings."

Little Bear ran to the fireplace where his six stockings hung, and he found a jar of honey in every one!

Then he went to his corner cupboard and took out a little round red cheese for Squeaky, a tiny box of sunflower seeds for Sparrow, a small bag of acorns for Squirrel and an orange for Owl.

He had been saving them all for himself, but now he wanted to give them to his
friends.

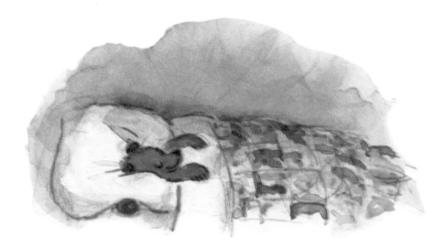

And *then* they had the party, and everyone ate as much as he could! After the party everyone went home. "How nice it is to have Christmas!" Little Bear said, as he got ready for bed.

And he put a jar of honey under his pillow—just in case he should wake up again and feel hungry before Spring.

The next moment Little Bear was sound asleep.